A JOURNEY TO THE CENTRE OF THE EARTH

OF THE

EARTH

JULES VERNE

Go down the crater of Sneffel, that the shadow of Scartaris softly touches before the beginning of July, brave traveller, and you will come to the centre of the earth. I did it.

Arne Saknussemm

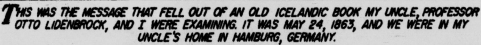

THIS WAS THE MESSAGE THAT FELL OUT OF AN OLD ICELANDIC BOOK MY UNCLE, PROFESSOR OTTO LIDENBROCK, AND I WERE EXAMINING. IT WAS MAY 24, 1863, AND WE WERE IN MY UNCLE'S HOME IN HAMBURG, GERMANY.

WHO IS ARNE SAKNUSSEMM, UNCLE?

HE WAS A GREAT ICELANDIC SCIENTIST, AXEL. HE LIVED IN THE SIXTEENTH CENTURY.

BUT WHAT DOES THIS MEAN? WHAT ARE SNEFFEL AND SCARTARIS?

SNEFFEL IS AN EXTINCT VOLCANO IN ICELAND. SCARTARIS IS THE NAME OF ONE OF ITS PEAKS.

AND WHAT'S THIS ABOUT THE BEGINNING OF JULY?

BEFORE THE BEGINNING OF JULY, SCARTARIS MUST CAST ITS SHADOW OVER THE OPENING OF THE CRATER THAT LED SAKNUSSEMM TO THE CENTRE OF THE EARTH.

BUT SUCH A JOURNEY WOULD BE IMPOSSIBLE! SCIENCE TELLS US THAT THE DEEPER YOU GO INTO THE EARTH, THE HOTTER IT BECOMES. AT THE CENTRE OF THE EARTH, IT MUST BE 20,000 DEGREES.

THAT THEORY HAS NEVER BEEN PROVEN. BUT, LIKE ARNE SAKNUSSEMM, LET US GO AND FIND OUT FOR OURSELVES.

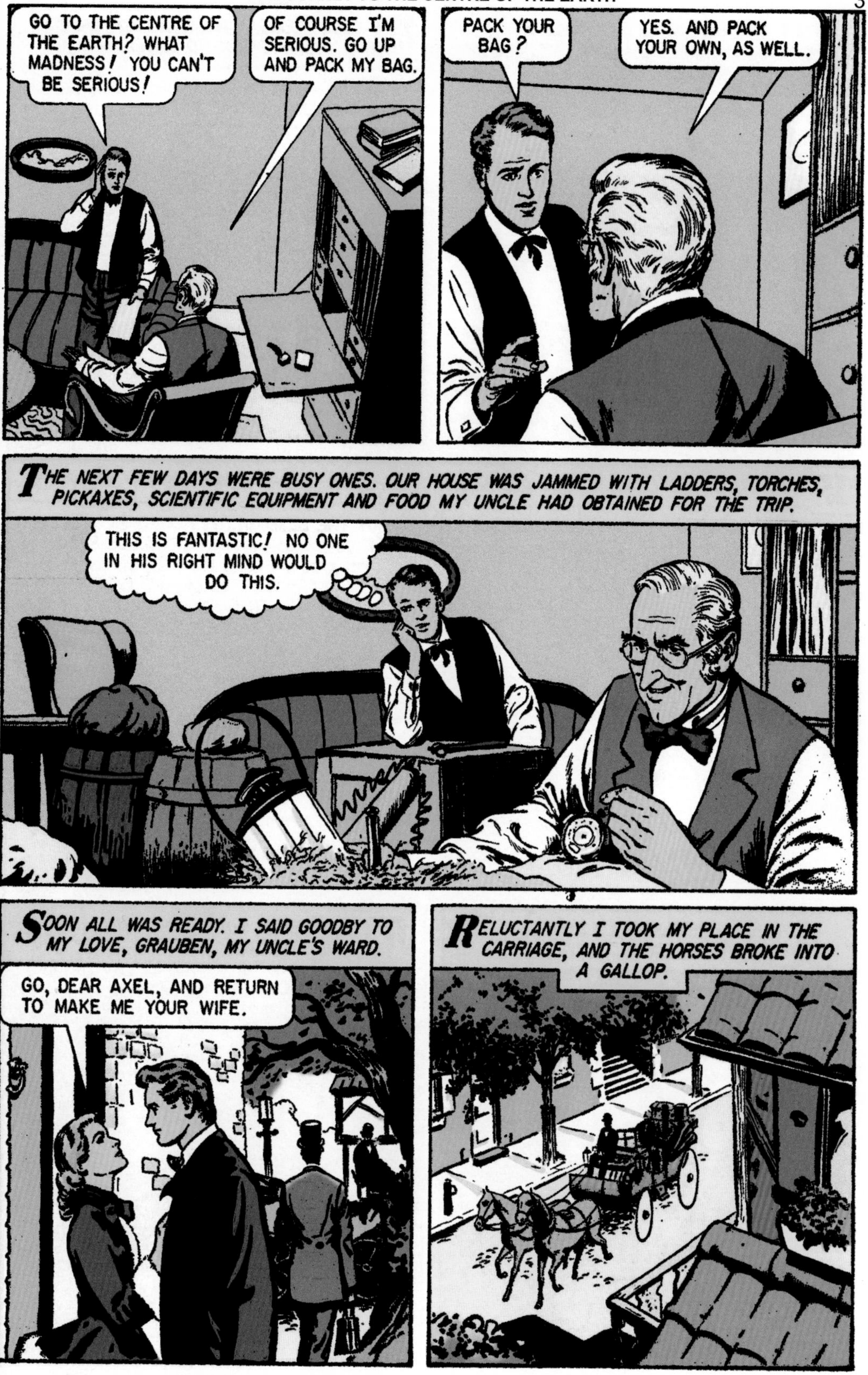
GO TO THE CENTRE OF THE EARTH? WHAT MADNESS! YOU CAN'T BE SERIOUS!
OF COURSE I'M SERIOUS. GO UP AND PACK MY BAG.
PACK YOUR BAG?
YES. AND PACK YOUR OWN, AS WELL.
THE NEXT FEW DAYS WERE BUSY ONES. OUR HOUSE WAS JAMMED WITH LADDERS, TORCHES, PICKAXES, SCIENTIFIC EQUIPMENT AND FOOD MY UNCLE HAD OBTAINED FOR THE TRIP.
THIS IS FANTASTIC! NO ONE IN HIS RIGHT MIND WOULD DO THIS.
SOON ALL WAS READY. I SAID GOODBY TO MY LOVE, GRAUBEN, MY UNCLE'S WARD.
GO, DEAR AXEL, AND RETURN TO MAKE ME YOUR WIFE.
RELUCTANTLY I TOOK MY PLACE IN THE CARRIAGE, AND THE HORSES BROKE INTO A GALLOP.

AFTER SEVERAL WEEKS OF TRAVEL BY CARRIAGE, TRAIN AND BOAT, WE FINALLY REACHED ICELAND.

THERE IS MOUNT SNEFFEL.

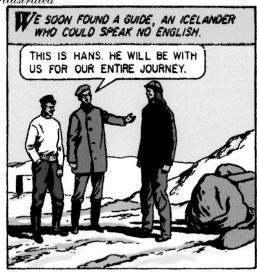

WE SOON FOUND A GUIDE, AN ICELANDER WHO COULD SPEAK NO ENGLISH.

THIS IS HANS. HE WILL BE WITH US FOR OUR ENTIRE JOURNEY.

WITH HANS IN THE LEAD, WE CLIMBED MOUNT SNEFFEL. WE WERE NEAR THE TOP WHEN . . .

MISTOUR!

IT IS A WHIRLWIND OF DUST AND STONES. COME QUICKLY!

WE SCRAMBLED OUT OF THE WAY JUST IN TIME.

HOURS LATER, WE REACHED THE TOP OF THE MOUNTAIN.

NOW, DOWN INTO THE VOLCANO!

WE MIGHT AS WELL CLIMB INTO A LOADED BLUNDERBUSS.

BUT I COULD NOT BACK OUT. SO DOWN WE WENT, CAREFULLY PICKING OUR WAY. WE SOON REACHED THE BOTTOM.

AXEL, LOOK! HERE IS THE NAME ARNE SAKNUSSEMM! WE ARE ON THE RIGHT TRACK.

ARNE SAKNUSSEMM

AND SEE, THERE ARE THREE OPENINGS. WE WILL GO DOWN THE ONE ON WHICH THE SHADOW OF SCARTARIS FALLS.

THE SHARP SHADOW OF SCARTARIS FELL ON THE CENTRAL OPENING.

THAT'S THE ONE! TO THE CENTRE OF THE EARTH!

ONE LOOK INTO THE HOLE MADE MY HAIR STAND ON END.

BUT USING A ROPE, WE CLIMBED DOWN.

TEN HOURS AND 2,800 FEET LATER . . .

WE ARE AT THE BOTTOM OF THE CHIMNEY. THERE IS A PASSAGE TO THE RIGHT, BUT WE SHALL INSPECT IT TOMORROW.

THE NEXT MORNING . . .

WELL, AXEL, DID YOU EVER PASS A MORE RESTFUL NIGHT? NOW GET UP. I AM ANXIOUS TO SEE WHAT IS AHEAD.

AFTER BREAKFAST, MY UNCLE LIT HIS LAMP AND PLUNGED INTO THE DARK CORRIDOR. I FOLLOWED, BUT ONLY AFTER TAKING A LAST LOOK AT THE SKIES OF ICELAND.

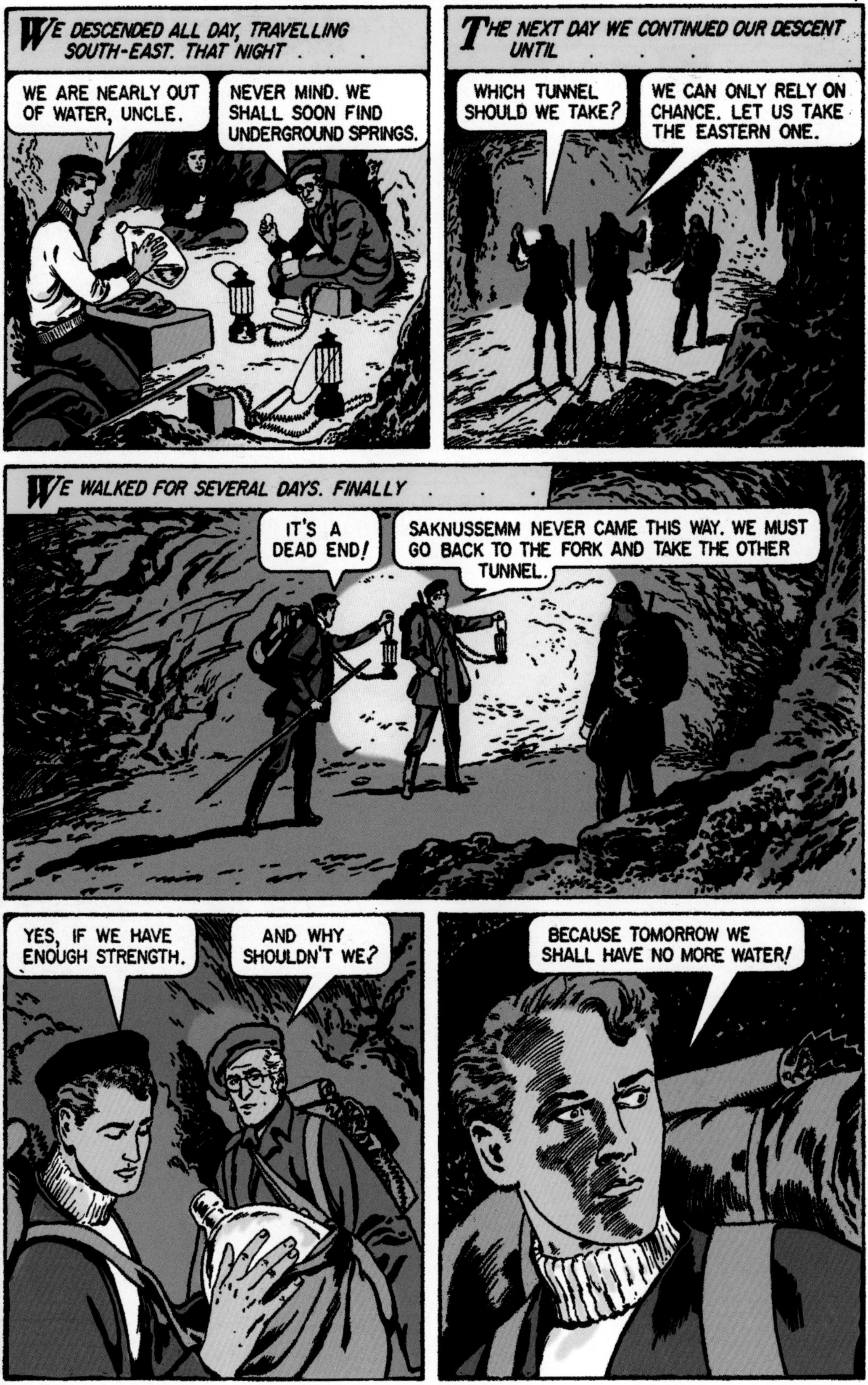
WE DESCENDED ALL DAY, TRAVELLING SOUTH-EAST. THAT NIGHT . . .
WE ARE NEARLY OUT OF WATER, UNCLE.
NEVER MIND. WE SHALL SOON FIND UNDERGROUND SPRINGS.
THE NEXT DAY WE CONTINUED OUR DESCENT UNTIL . . .
WHICH TUNNEL SHOULD WE TAKE?
WE CAN ONLY RELY ON CHANCE. LET US TAKE THE EASTERN ONE.
WE WALKED FOR SEVERAL DAYS. FINALLY . . .
IT'S A DEAD END!
SAKNUSSEMM NEVER CAME THIS WAY. WE MUST GO BACK TO THE FORK AND TAKE THE OTHER TUNNEL.
YES, IF WE HAVE ENOUGH STRENGTH.
AND WHY SHOULDN'T WE?
BECAUSE TOMORROW WE SHALL HAVE NO MORE WATER!

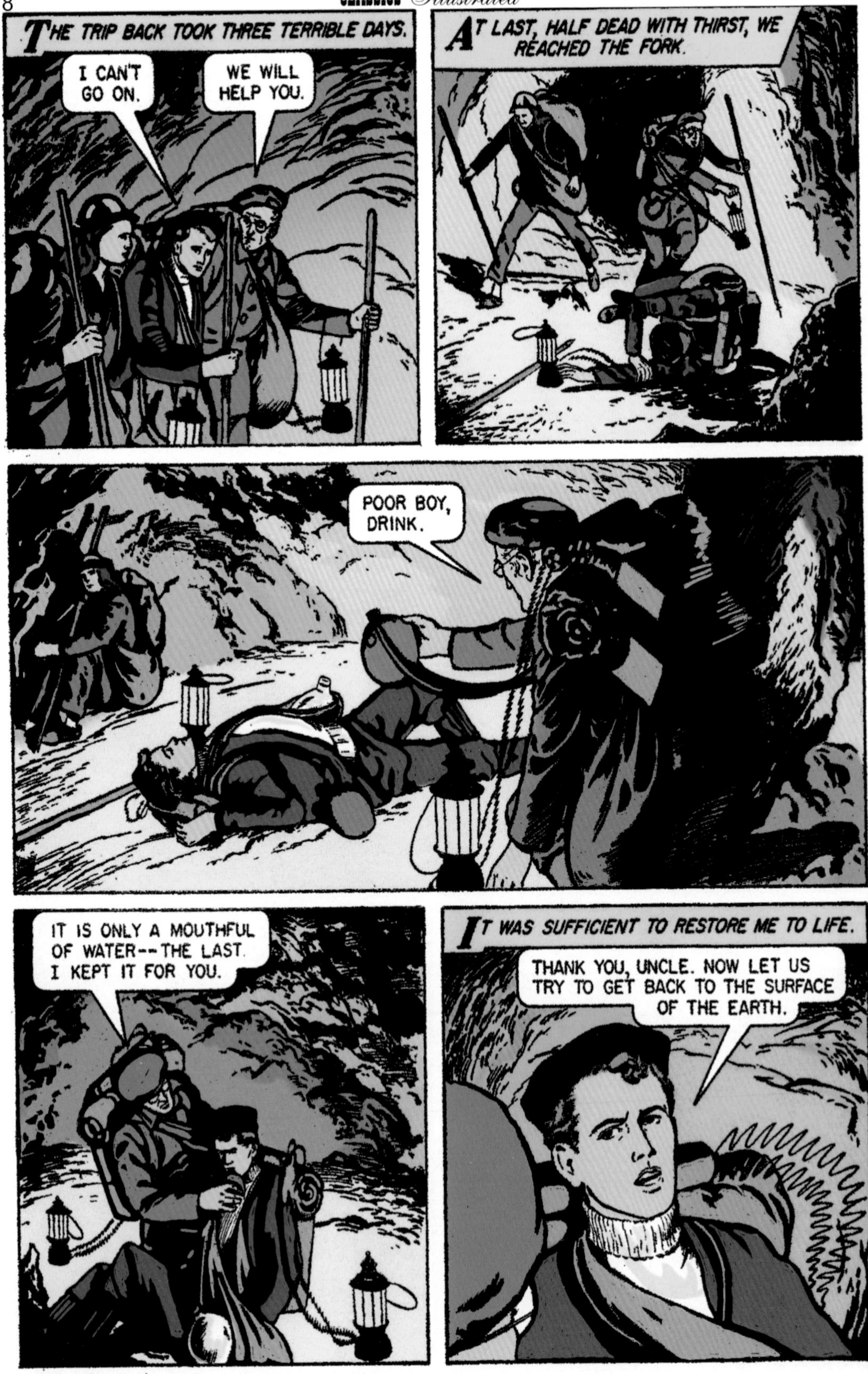
THE TRIP BACK TOOK THREE TERRIBLE DAYS.
I CAN'T GO ON.
WE WILL HELP YOU.
AT LAST, HALF DEAD WITH THIRST, WE REACHED THE FORK.
POOR BOY, DRINK.
IT IS ONLY A MOUTHFUL OF WATER--THE LAST. I KEPT IT FOR YOU.
IT WAS SUFFICIENT TO RESTORE ME TO LIFE.
THANK YOU, UNCLE. NOW LET US TRY TO GET BACK TO THE SURFACE OF THE EARTH.

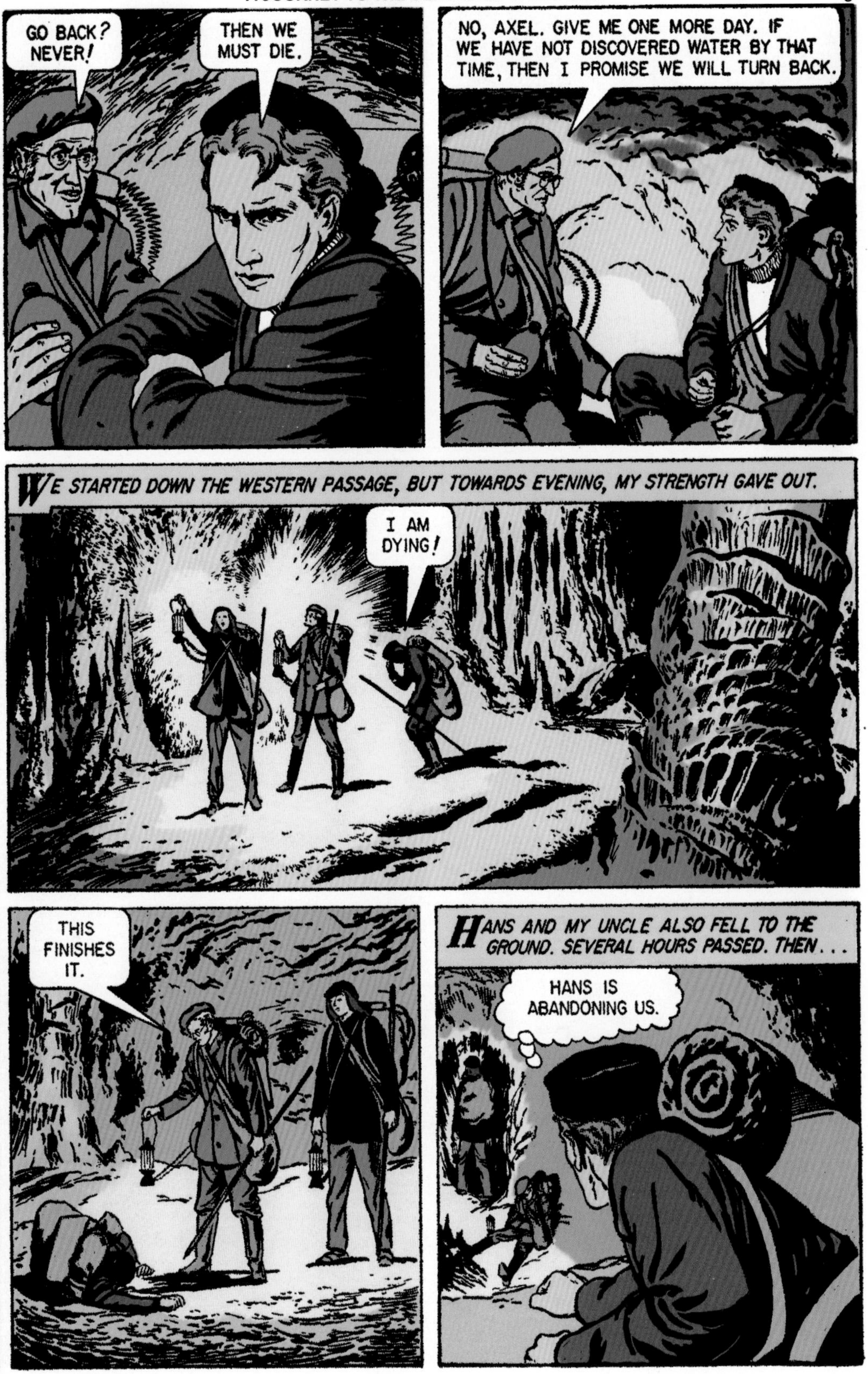
GO BACK? NEVER!
THEN WE MUST DIE.
NO, AXEL. GIVE ME ONE MORE DAY. IF WE HAVE NOT DISCOVERED WATER BY THAT TIME, THEN I PROMISE WE WILL TURN BACK.
WE STARTED DOWN THE WESTERN PASSAGE, BUT TOWARDS EVENING, MY STRENGTH GAVE OUT.
I AM DYING!
THIS FINISHES IT.
HANS AND MY UNCLE ALSO FELL TO THE GROUND. SEVERAL HOURS PASSED. THEN . . .
HANS IS ABANDONING US.

BUT SOON HE RETURNED.

VATTEN. NEDAT.

HE SAYS THERE IS WATER DOWN BELOW COME!

SOON WE COULD HEAR AN UNUSUAL SOUND ON THE OTHER SIDE OF THE WALL.

AN UNDERGROUND RIVER IS RUNNING CLOSE BESIDE US.

HANS TOOK UP HIS PICK AND

WE'RE SAVED!

YES. THE WATER WILL FLOW BESIDE US DOWN THE PASSAGE, SO WE WILL NOT BE WITHOUT IT AGAIN.

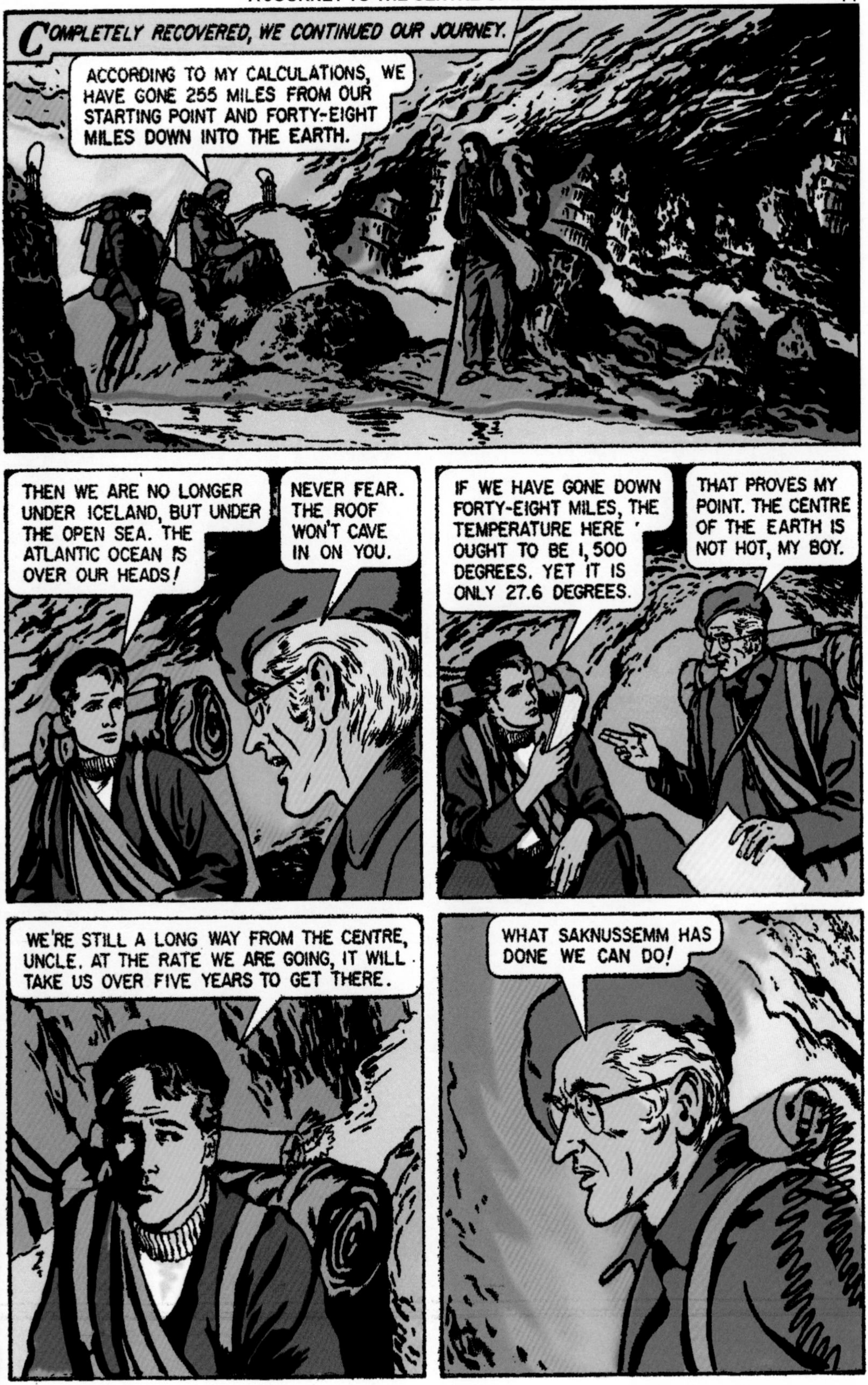
COMPLETELY RECOVERED, WE CONTINUED OUR JOURNEY.
ACCORDING TO MY CALCULATIONS, WE HAVE GONE 255 MILES FROM OUR STARTING POINT AND FORTY-EIGHT MILES DOWN INTO THE EARTH.
THEN WE ARE NO LONGER UNDER ICELAND, BUT UNDER THE OPEN SEA. THE ATLANTIC OCEAN IS OVER OUR HEADS!
NEVER FEAR. THE ROOF WON'T CAVE IN ON YOU.
IF WE HAVE GONE DOWN FORTY-EIGHT MILES, THE TEMPERATURE HERE OUGHT TO BE 1,500 DEGREES. YET IT IS ONLY 27.6 DEGREES.
THAT PROVES MY POINT. THE CENTRE OF THE EARTH IS NOT HOT, MY BOY.
WE'RE STILL A LONG WAY FROM THE CENTRE, UNCLE. AT THE RATE WE ARE GOING, IT WILL TAKE US OVER FIVE YEARS TO GET THERE.
WHAT SAKNUSSEMM HAS DONE WE CAN DO!

WE RESUMED OUR DESCENT. ONE DAY, I TOOK THE LEAD.

ALL AT ONCE, I TURNED TO SPEAK TO THE OTHERS.

HELLO! WHERE ARE THEY?

I MUST HAVE BEEN GOING TOO FAST. I'LL WALK BACK AND MEET THEM.

UNCLE! HANS!

THERE WAS NO ANSWER. A SHIVER RAN THROUGH MY BODY.

THERE IS ONLY ONE ROUTE, AND IT IS MARKED BY THE RIVER. I HAVE ONLY TO FOLLOW THE RIVER BACK.

I CROUCHED DOWN TO PUT MY HANDS IN THE RIVER.

IT IS NOT HERE!

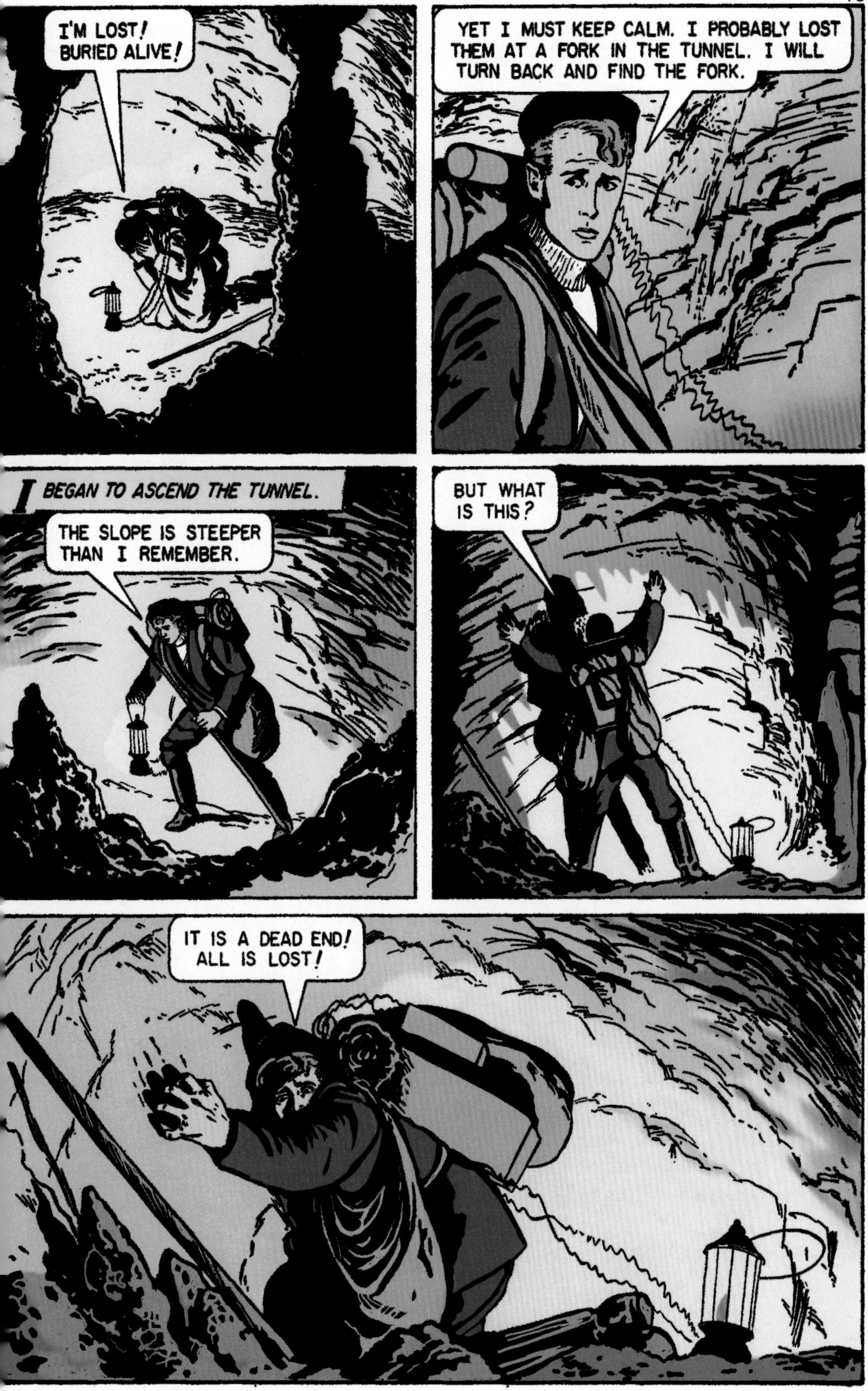
I'M LOST! BURIED ALIVE!
YET I MUST KEEP CALM. I PROBABLY LOST THEM AT A FORK IN THE TUNNEL. I WILL TURN BACK AND FIND THE FORK.
I BEGAN TO ASCEND THE TUNNEL.
THE SLOPE IS STEEPER THAN I REMEMBER.
BUT WHAT IS THIS?
IT IS A DEAD END! ALL IS LOST!

THEN A NEW TERROR POSSESSED ME.

MY LAMP IS GOING OUT. I MUST HAVE DAMAGED IT.

I WATCHED THE CURRENT FADE.

WHEN I WAS ALONE IN THE ABSOLUTE DARKNESS, I LOST MY HEAD. I BROKE INTO MAD FLIGHT.

I SMASHED INTO ROCKS, FELL, SCRAMBLED BLEEDING TO MY FEET.

FINALLY, I COLLAPSED IN AN UNCONSCIOUS HEAP.

WHEN I CAME TO, I TRIED TO GET UP, BUT I SUCCEEDED ONLY IN ROLLING OVER.

SUDDENLY I SEEMED TO HEAR A FEW MUFFLED WORDS.

IT IS A HALLUCINATION!

NO, SOMEONE IS TALKING. IT MUST BE UNCLE AND HANS, FOR WHAT OTHER MEN WOULD BE BURIED NINETY MILES UNDERGROUND?

THIS TUNNEL MUST HAVE SOME PECULIAR ABILITY TO CONDUCT SOUND. PERHAPS THEY WILL BE ABLE TO HEAR ME.

UNCLE LIDENBROCK!

AXEL! IS THAT YOU?

YES! YES!

WHERE ARE YOU?

LOST IN THE BLACKEST DARKNESS. I WILL TRY TO COME TO YOU, BUT SHOULD I GO UP OR DOWN THE TUNNEL?

GO DOWN THE TUNNEL, FOR WE HAVE COME TO AN IMMENSE OPEN PLACE INTO WHICH SEVERAL TUNNELS RUN. YOURS MUST LEAD HERE. WALK, CRAWL, SLIDE DOWN THE TUNNEL, AND YOU WILL FIND US WAITING FOR YOU.

I STARTED OFF, SOMETIMES WALKING, SOMETIMES CRAWLING.

SUDDENLY, I FELT MYSELF FALLING. MY HEAD STRUCK A ROCK AND I LOST CONSCIOUSNESS.

WHEN I AWOKE . . .

HE IS ALIVE! THANK GOD!

UNCLE, I AM SO GLAD TO SEE YOU AND HANS AGAIN.

BUT WHERE ARE WE? I SEEM TO SEE LIGHT AND HEAR THE SOUND OF WIND AND SURF.

I CANNOT EXPLAIN IT, BUT YOU WILL SEE FOR YOURSELF WHEN YOU ARE WELL ENOUGH TO GO INTO THE OPEN AIR.

OPEN AIR?

YES. IT MIGHT CAUSE YOU TO HAVE A RELAPSE, WHICH WOULD DELAY OUR CROSSING.

CROSSING?

YES. WE WILL SET SAIL TOMORROW.

BURSTING WITH CURIOSITY, I INSISTED ON GOING TO THE EXIT OF THE GROTTO.

ONCE THERE, I STARED IN AMAZEMENT.

BEFORE ME WAS A TREMENDOUS CAVERN WITH A REAL UNDERGROUND OCEAN WHICH STRETCHED FURTHER THAN THE EYE COULD SEE.

IT'S FANTASTIC! WHERE DOES THE LIGHT COME FROM?

I IMAGINE IT IS OF ELECTRICAL ORIGIN.

ARE YOU STRONG ENOUGH FOR A LITTLE WALK?

I SHOULD LIKE NOTHING BETTER.

WE STROLLED ALONG THE SHORE.

WHAT ARE THOSE STRANGE TREES?

THEY ARE NOT TREES, BUT MUSHROOMS. THEY HAVE GROWN SO TALL BECAUSE OF THE WARMTH AND DAMPNESS DOWN HERE.

THE SAME THING HAS HAPPENED TO THESE. THEY ARE HUMBLE SHRUBS IN THE UPPER WORLD, BUT LOOK AT THEM HERE!

AND SEE WHAT ELSE WE FIND. THE BONES OF PREHISTORIC ANIMALS ARE SCATTERED OVER THE GROUND.

YES. HUGE, TERRIBLE MONSTERS ONCE LIVED ON THESE SHORES.

PERHAPS ONE OF THEM IS STILL WANDERING ABOUT.

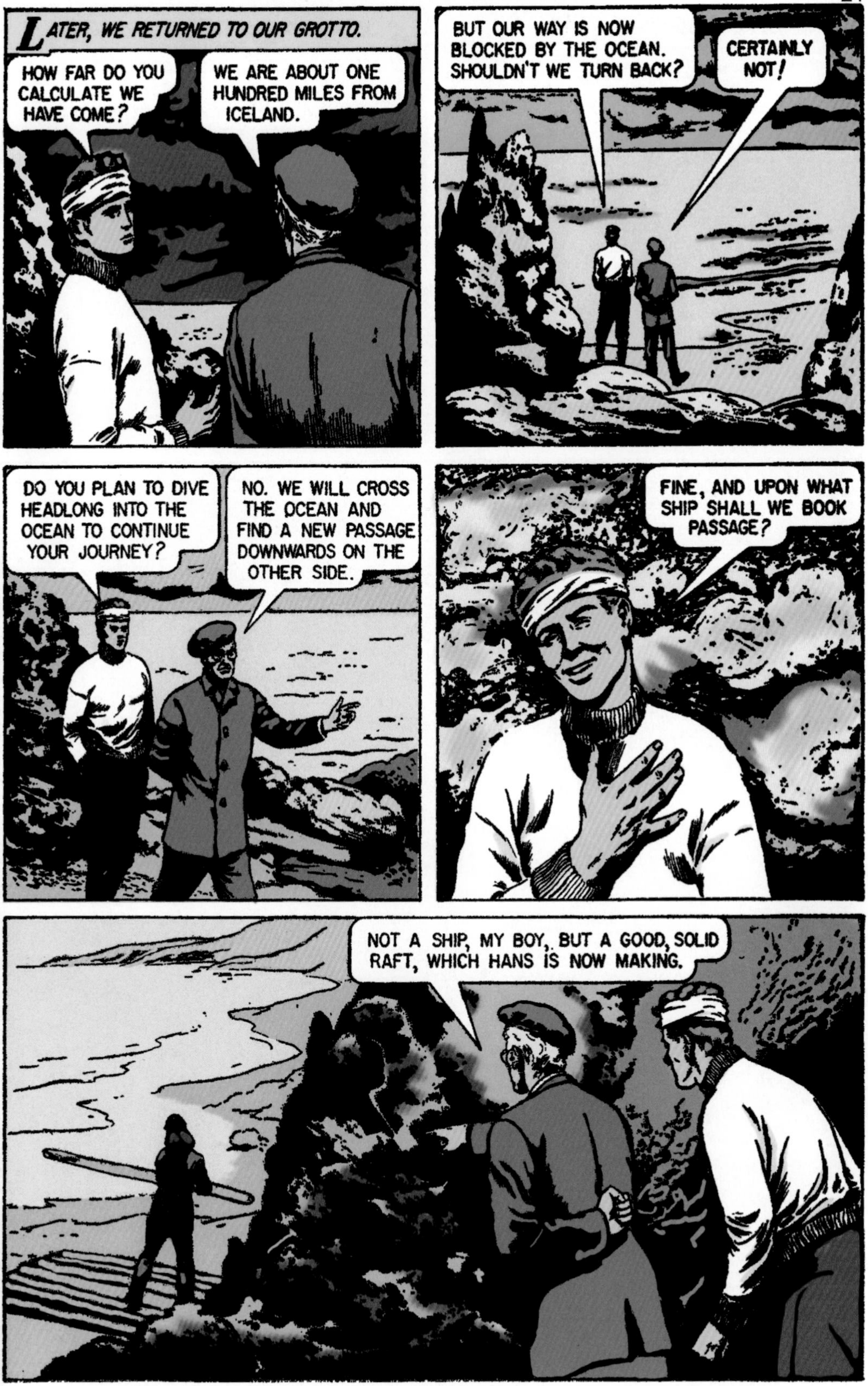
LATER, WE RETURNED TO OUR GROTTO.
HOW FAR DO YOU CALCULATE WE HAVE COME?
WE ARE ABOUT ONE HUNDRED MILES FROM ICELAND.
BUT OUR WAY IS NOW BLOCKED BY THE OCEAN. SHOULDN'T WE TURN BACK?
CERTAINLY NOT!
DO YOU PLAN TO DIVE HEADLONG INTO THE OCEAN TO CONTINUE YOUR JOURNEY?
NO. WE WILL CROSS THE OCEAN AND FIND A NEW PASSAGE DOWNWARDS ON THE OTHER SIDE.
FINE, AND UPON WHAT SHIP SHALL WE BOOK PASSAGE?
NOT A SHIP, MY BOY, BUT A GOOD, SOLID RAFT, WHICH HANS IS NOW MAKING.

AND THE NEXT MORNING . . .

CAST OFF!

A STEADY WIND BLEW US QUICKLY OUT TO SEA.

AT THIS RATE IT WON'T BE LONG BEFORE WE REACH THE OTHER SIDE.

AT NOON, HANS TOSSED OVER A FISHING LINE. SOON . . .

WE EXAMINED THE FISH.

IT BELONGS TO A FAMILY THAT BECAME EXTINCT OVER ONE HUNDRED MILLION YEARS AGO!

WELL, IT WILL BE A WELCOME ADDITION TO OUR DINNER MENU, ANYWAY.

OUR JOURNEY WENT WELL, BUT AFTER SEVERAL DAYS MY UNCLE BEGAN TO GROW RESTLESS.

HAVE PATIENCE, UNCLE. WE ARE MAKING GOOD PROGRESS.

IT IS NOT THAT OUR PROGRESS IS TOO SLOW, BUT THAT THE SEA IS TOO BIG.

WE HAVE TRAVELLED MORE THAN THREE HUNDRED MILES, YET THE OPPOSITE SHORE IS NOT EVEN IN SIGHT. WE ARE LOSING TIME BECAUSE WE ARE NOT MAKING ANY PROGRESS DOWNWARDS.

TO TRY TO FIND OUT THE DEPTH OF THE SEA, WE LET DOWN OUR HEAVIEST PICK ON A ROPE. WHEN WE PULLED IT IN . . .

WHAT DO YOU MAKE OF THESE STRANGE MARKS?

TEETH!

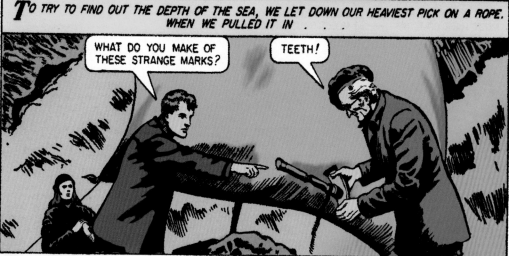

THE PICK IS BITTEN HALF THROUGH. PERHAPS WE HAVE DISTURBED SOME MARINE ANIMAL IN ITS LAIR.

I CHECKED OUR GUNS, THEN TURNED TO STARE FEARFULLY AT THE OCEAN.

FINALLY I FELL ASLEEP, BUT I WAS AWAKENED BY A TREMENDOUS JOLT.

THAT COLOSSAL PORPOISE MUST HAVE COME UP UNDER US.

AND THERE'S A MONSTROUS CROCODILE! AND A WHALE!

HANS TRIED TO CHANGE COURSE AND FLEE BUT . . .

OUR WAY IS BLOCKED BY THAT GIGANTIC TURTLE AND THAT SEA SERPENT!

THEY ARE COMING NEARER. THEY WILL SOON BE UPON US!

BUT THE MONSTERS PASSED US AND ATTACKED EACH OTHER WITH INDESCRIBABLE FURY.

WE WATCHED, HORRIFIED.

HOW MANY ARE THERE?

THERE ARE ONLY TWO.

BUT WE SAW MANY.

NO. ONE IS AN ICHTHYOSAURUS, WHICH HAS THE BACK OF A PORPOISE, THE HEAD OF A CROCODILE AND THE FINS OF A WHALE. THE OTHER IS A PLESIOSAURUS, A SERPENT WITH A SHELL LIKE A TURTLES.

FOR TWO HOURS THE ANIMALS FOUGHT, CHURNING UP MOUNTAINOUS WAVES WHICH THREATENED TO CAPSIZE US.

FINALLY, LOCKED TOGETHER, THEY DISAPPEARED BENEATH THE SURFACE OF THE SEA.

THEN AN ENORMOUS HEAD SHOT UP.

THE PLESIOSAURUS IS MORTALLY WOUNDED.

IN A FEW MINUTES . . .

IT'S DEAD. LET US HOPE ITS CONQUEROR HAS RETURNED TO HIS SUBMARINE HOME.

WE DREW RAPIDLY AWAY FROM THE SCENE OF THE STRUGGLE. SEVERAL DAYS PASSED QUIETLY. THEN . . .

THE AIR IS FULL OF ELECTRICITY, AND THE CLOUDS ARE BUILDING UP. WE ARE IN FOR A STORM.

FOR A TIME, THE RAFT FLOATED MOTIONLESS ON A DULL SEA.

FINALLY, THE STORM HIT.

THE SEA BEGAN TO CHURN AND THE RAFT FLEW TOWARDS THE HORIZON.

CLAPS OF THUNDER FOLLOWED BOLTS OF LIGHTNING.

COLUMNS OF WATER LEAPED UP AND FELL BACK AS FOAM.

WAVES WASHED OVER OUR HEADS.

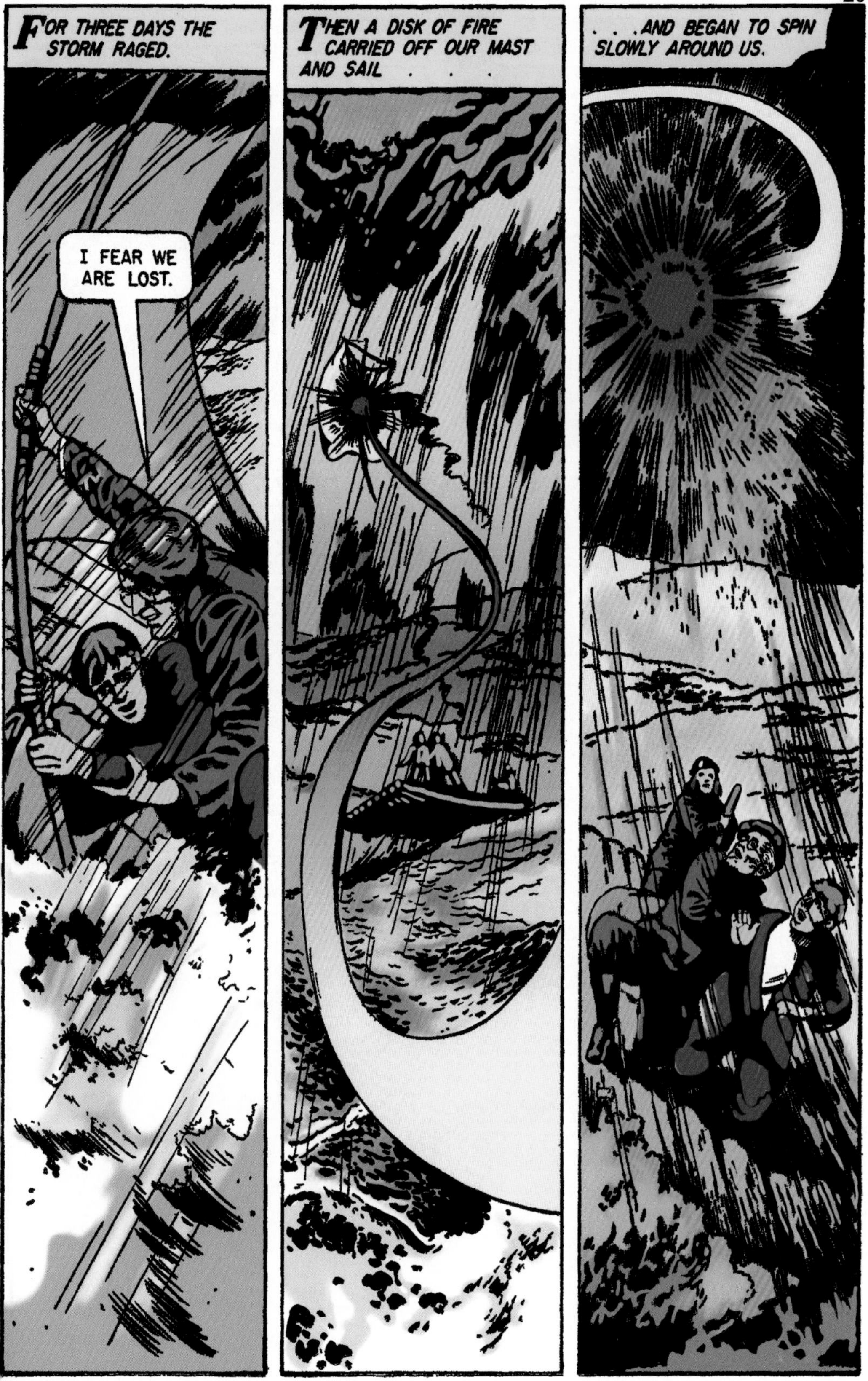
FOR THREE DAYS THE STORM RAGED.
I FEAR WE ARE LOST.
THEN A DISK OF FIRE CARRIED OFF OUR MAST AND SAIL . . .
. . . AND BEGAN TO SPIN SLOWLY AROUND US.

WE SAT FROZEN WITH TERROR AS IT LIGHTLY TOUCHED OUR GUNPOWDER.

WE WILL BE BLOWN UP!

BUT IT MOVED AWAY AND CAME TOWARDS MY FOOT.

I SNATCHED MY FOOT AWAY JUST IN TIME.

THEN I FAINTED. WHEN I CAME TO . . .

THERE IS A NEW NOISE. IT SOUNDS LIKE THE SEAS ARE BREAKING UPON ROCKS.

AND SOON WE WERE FLUNG UPON A SHORE.

WE CRAWLED UNDER SOME SHELTERING ROCKS AND FELL ASLEEP. WHEN WE AWOKE, THE STORM HAD PASSED.

SEE, MY BOY, IT IS A BEAUTIFUL DAY!

WELL, UNCLE, YOU SEEM HAPPY THIS MORNING.

I AM, INDEED. WE HAVE COME TO THE END OF THE SEA AND CAN ONCE MORE MAKE OUR WAY DOWN TO THE CENTRE OF THE EARTH.

BUT HAVEN'T ALL OF OUR PROVISIONS AND SUPPLIES BEEN LOST?

NO. HANS HAS MANAGED TO SAVE MOST OF THEM.

WHERE DO YOU THINK WE ARE NOW, UNCLE?

UNDER THE MEDITERRANEAN SEA.

BUT BEFORE WE CONTINUE OUR JOURNEY, WE WILL HAVE TO EXPLORE THIS COAST TO FIND THE PASSAGE THAT WILL LEAD US DOWNWARDS.

WE WALKED INLAND AND PRESENTLY FOUND OURSELVES ON A PLAIN STREWN WITH THE BONES OF EXTINCT ANIMALS.

IT'S ASTOUNDING, AXEL. HERE IS A WHOLE HISTORY OF ANIMAL LIFE.

AND LOOK! HERE IS A HUMAN SKULL!

WE KEPT WALKING UNTIL WE CAME TO A HUGE FOREST.

LET'S GO BACK. THERE MIGHT BE A LIVE ANIMAL ABOUT.

NONSENSE, COME ON!

I FOLLOWED FEARFULLY. THEN . . .

UNCLE, LOOK OVER THERE!

IT WAS A HERD OF GIANT MAMMOTHS.

COME, LET'S HAVE A CLOSER LOOK.

NO. IT'S TOO DANGEROUS. NO MAN WOULD DARE GO NEAR THEM.

NO MAN? BUT YOU ARE MISTAKEN, AXEL. LOOK OVER THERE!

IT WAS A PREHISTORIC MAN--AT LEAST TWELVE FEET TALL.

WE MUST GET AWAY BEFORE HE SEES US.

WE RAN LIKE MADMEN UNTIL WE REACHED THE SHORE.

THERE WE RESUMED OUR SEARCH FOR A PASSAGE THAT WOULD LEAD DOWNWARDS.

THERE SHOULD BE ONE HERE SOMEWHERE. YET I SEE NOTHING.

BUT I SEE SOMETHING!

I PICKED UP A RUSTY KNIFE.

HOW STRANGE! IT IS A KNIFE SUCH AS ICELANDERS OFTEN CARRY, BUT IT MUST BE SEVERAL HUNDRED YEARS OLD.

HOW DID IT GET HERE, UNLESS . . . UNLESS SOMEONE WAS HERE BEFORE US.

OF COURSE! IT BELONGED TO ARNE SAKNUSSEMM! PERHAPS HE USED IT TO CARVE A MESSAGE!

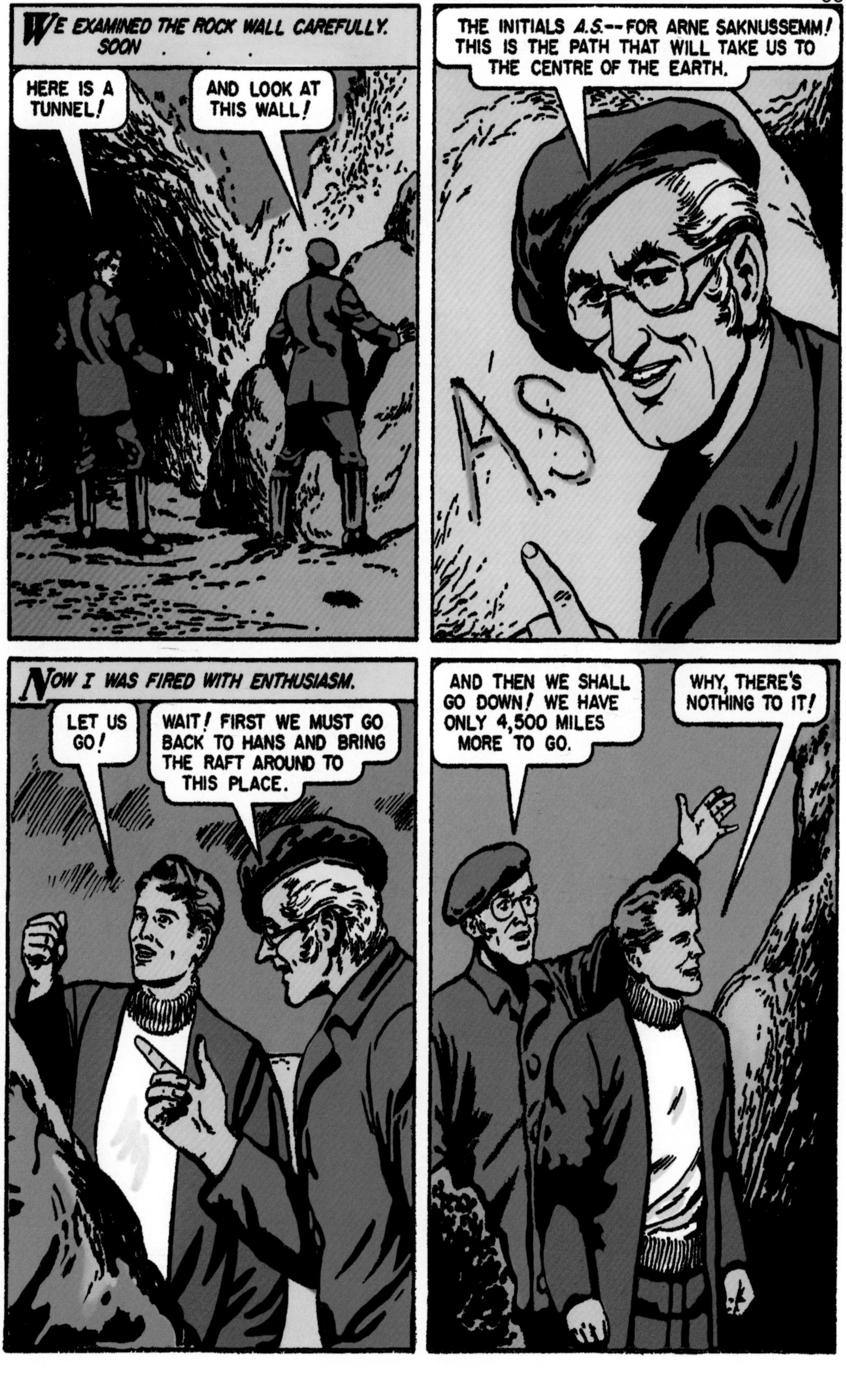
WE EXAMINED THE ROCK WALL CAREFULLY. SOON . . .
HERE IS A TUNNEL!
AND LOOK AT THIS WALL!
THE INITIALS A.S.-- FOR ARNE SAKNUSSEMM! THIS IS THE PATH THAT WILL TAKE US TO THE CENTRE OF THE EARTH.
A.S.
NOW I WAS FIRED WITH ENTHUSIASM.
LET US GO!
WAIT! FIRST WE MUST GO BACK TO HANS AND BRING THE RAFT AROUND TO THIS PLACE.
AND THEN WE SHALL GO DOWN! WE HAVE ONLY 4,500 MILES MORE TO GO.
WHY, THERE'S NOTHING TO IT!

WE RETURNED TO HANS, LOADED THE RAFT AND SAILED BACK TO OUR TUNNEL.

NOW LET US EXAMINE THIS NEW PASSAGE.

WE HAD GONE ONLY A FEW STEPS WHEN...

THE WAY IS BLOCKED!

WE SEARCHED FOR ANOTHER PASSAGEWAY BUT WE FOUND NONE.

WAS SAKNUSSEMM ALSO STOPPED BY THIS ROCK?

NO. IT MUST HAVE FALLEN AND CLOSED THE TUNNEL LONG AFTER SAKNUSSEMM PASSED THIS WAY.

THEN WE MUST OPEN IT—PERHAPS WITH A PICKAXE.

NO. IT'S TOO HARD FOR A PICKAXE.

LET'S BLOW IT TO PIECES WITH GUNPOWDER!

WE HOLLOWED OUT A HOLE IN THE ROCK FOR THE GUNPOWDER AND MADE A LONG FUSE.

AFTER YOU LIGHT THE FUSE, JOIN US ON THE RAFT. WE WILL HEAD OUT TO SEA TO AVOID ANY DANGER FROM THE EXPLOSION.

MY UNCLE AND HANS GOT ON THE RAFT. I LIT THE FUSE AND RACED TOWARDS THEM.

SAFE AT SEA, WE WAITED BREATHLESSLY.

THREE, TWO, ONE . . . NOW!

WITH A GREAT ROAR THE SHAPE OF THE CLIFF CHANGED AND A HUGE HOLE OPENED ALONG THE SHORE.

WE WERE SWEPT INTO THE HOLE AND FELT OURSELVES SWIRLING DOWN INTO DARKNESS.

FOR SEVERAL HOURS WE WERE CARRIED ALONG AT A TREMENDOUS SPEED.

SUDDENLY THE RAFT STOPPED, AND A FLOOD OF WATER SPILLED OVER US.

HOWEVER, IN A FEW SECONDS WE WERE ONCE MORE IN FRESH AIR.

THEN . . .

WE ARE GOING UP.

WHAT? ARE YOU SURE?

YES. WE ARE IN A SORT OF A WELL. THE WATER, HAVING REACHED BOTTOM, IS NOW GOING UP AGAIN, AND WE ARE GOING UP WITH IT.

BUT WHERE WILL IT TAKE US?

I DON'T KNOW. AS WE MUST BE READY FOR ANYTHING, LET US MAKE OURSELVES STRONGER BY EATING SOMETHING.

I QUICKLY SEARCHED THE RAFT.

OUR PROVISIONS ARE GONE. THERE IS ONLY SOME DRIED MEAT FOR THE THREE OF US.

LET US EAT IT, THEN. IT MAY BE OUR LAST MEAL, BUT IT WILL GIVE US STRENGTH TO MEET THE END.

WE ATE SILENTLY. SOMEWHAT REVIVED, I BEGAN TO LOOK ABOUT.

UNCLE, THIS ROCK IS HOT!

AND THE WATER BENEATH US IS BOILING!

WE HEARD SOUNDS LIKE DISTANT EXPLOSIONS.

THE WALLS ARE SHAKING!

UNCLE, WE ARE LOST!

NOW WHAT IS THE MATTER WITH YOU?

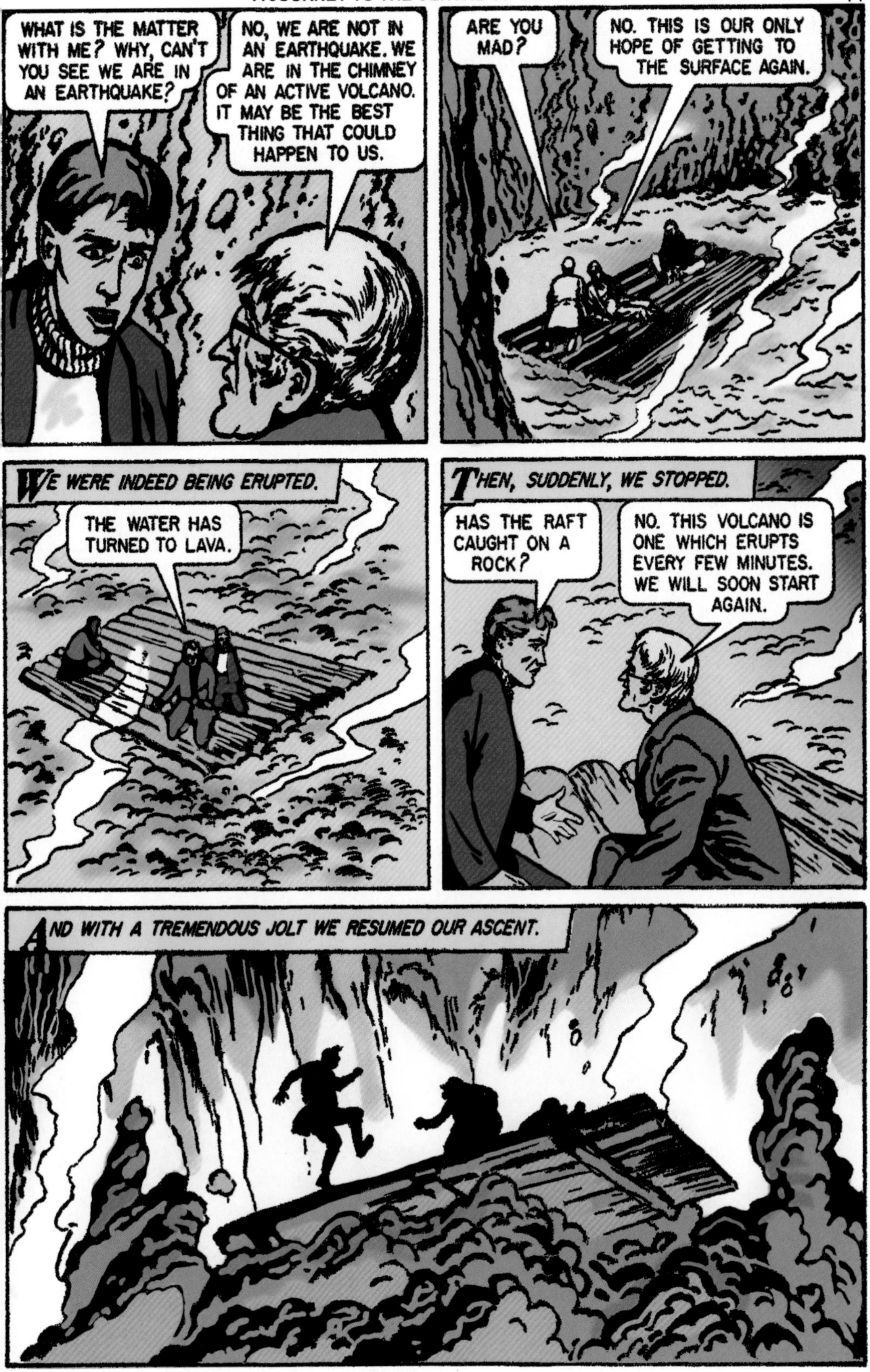
WHAT IS THE MATTER WITH ME? WHY, CAN'T YOU SEE WE ARE IN AN EARTHQUAKE?
NO, WE ARE NOT IN AN EARTHQUAKE. WE ARE IN THE CHIMNEY OF AN ACTIVE VOLCANO. IT MAY BE THE BEST THING THAT COULD HAPPEN TO US.
ARE YOU MAD?
NO. THIS IS OUR ONLY HOPE OF GETTING TO THE SURFACE AGAIN.
WE WERE INDEED BEING ERUPTED.
THE WATER HAS TURNED TO LAVA.
THEN, SUDDENLY, WE STOPPED.
HAS THE RAFT CAUGHT ON A ROCK?
NO. THIS VOLCANO IS ONE WHICH ERUPTS EVERY FEW MINUTES. WE WILL SOON START AGAIN.
AND WITH A TREMENDOUS JOLT WE RESUMED OUR ASCENT.

THE RUSH OF STIFLING AIR LEFT ME BREATHLESS.

SHOCK FOLLOWED SHOCK, AND I BEGAN TO LOSE MY SENSES.

THE RAFT SEEMED TO BE TURNING ROUND AND ROUND WITH ROARING FIRE ON EVERY SIDE.

THE LAST THING I REMEMBER WAS HANS' FACE, LIT BY THE BRIGHT RED OF THE FIRE. THEN I LOST CONSCIOUSNESS.

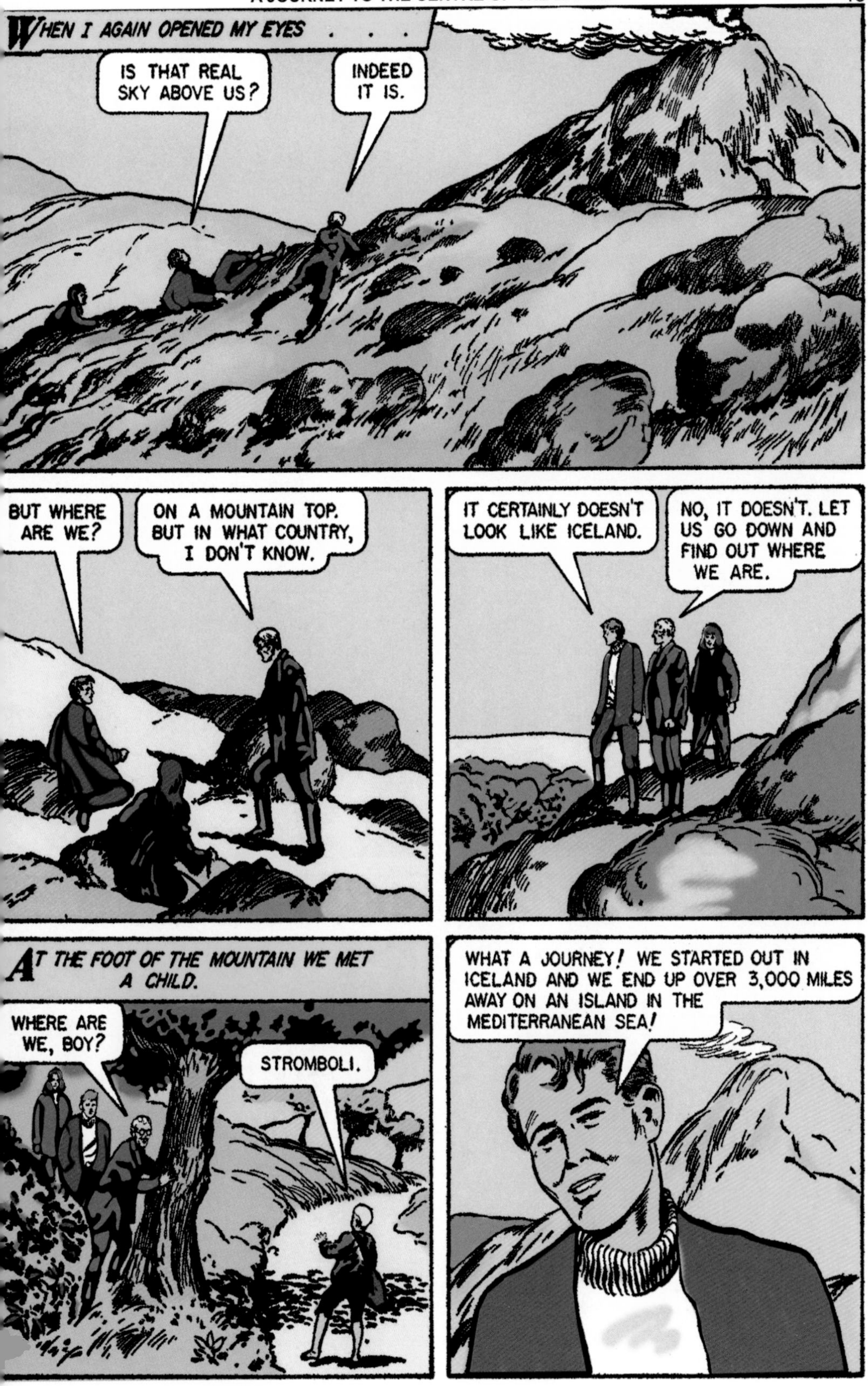
WHEN I AGAIN OPENED MY EYES . . .
IS THAT REAL SKY ABOVE US?
INDEED IT IS.
BUT WHERE ARE WE?
ON A MOUNTAIN TOP. BUT IN WHAT COUNTRY, I DON'T KNOW.
IT CERTAINLY DOESN'T LOOK LIKE ICELAND.
NO, IT DOESN'T. LET US GO DOWN AND FIND OUT WHERE WE ARE.
AT THE FOOT OF THE MOUNTAIN WE MET A CHILD.
WHERE ARE WE, BOY?
STROMBOLI.
WHAT A JOURNEY! WE STARTED OUT IN ICELAND AND WE END UP OVER 3,000 MILES AWAY ON AN ISLAND IN THE MEDITERRANEAN SEA!

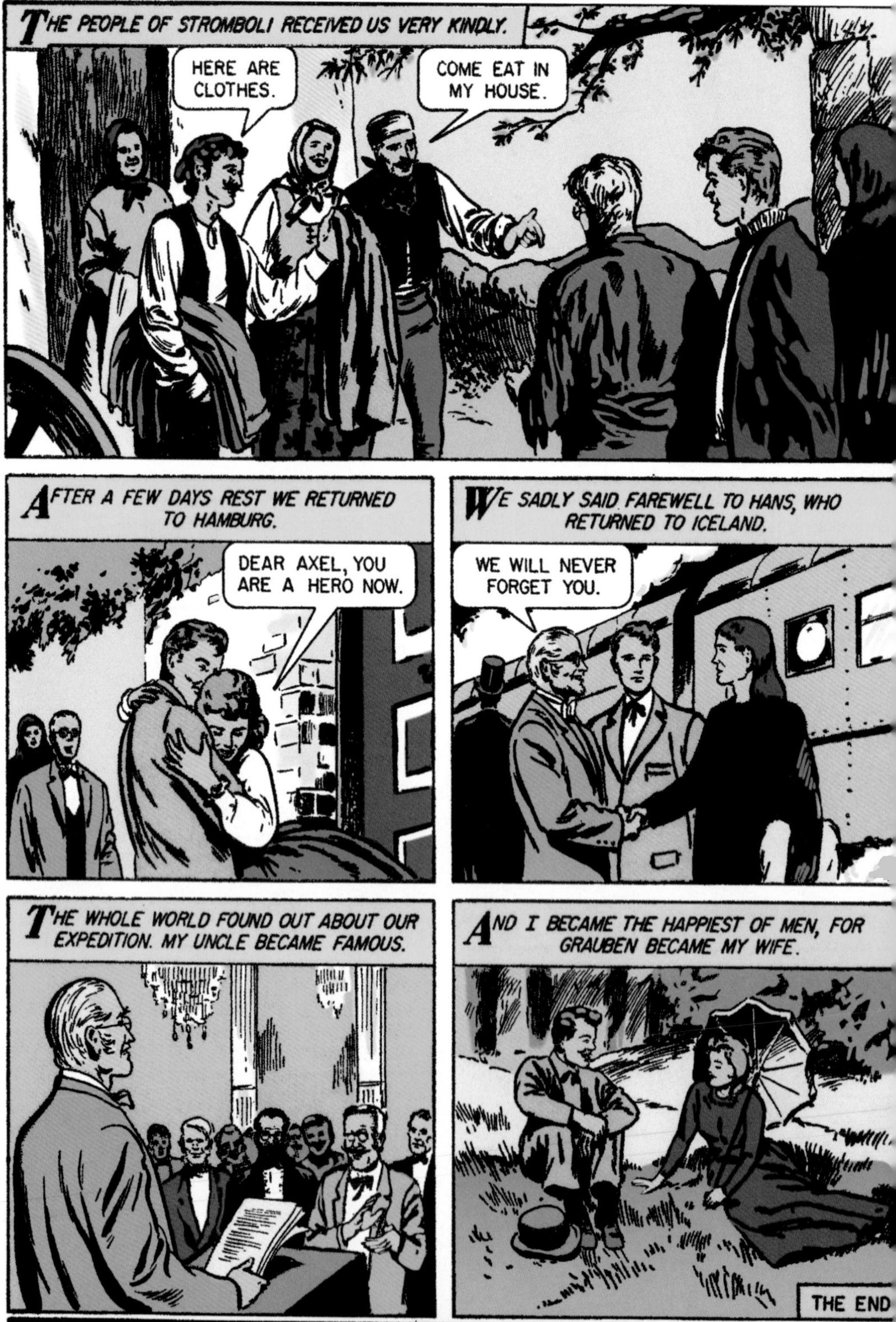
THE PEOPLE OF STROMBOLI RECEIVED US VERY KINDLY.
HERE ARE CLOTHES.
COME EAT IN MY HOUSE.
AFTER A FEW DAYS REST WE RETURNED TO HAMBURG.
DEAR AXEL, YOU ARE A HERO NOW.
WE SADLY SAID FAREWELL TO HANS, WHO RETURNED TO ICELAND.
WE WILL NEVER FORGET YOU.
THE WHOLE WORLD FOUND OUT ABOUT OUR EXPEDITION. MY UNCLE BECAME FAMOUS.
AND I BECAME THE HAPPIEST OF MEN, FOR GRAUBEN BECAME MY WIFE.
THE END

NOW THAT YOU HAVE READ THE CLASSICS *Illustrated* EDITION, DON'T MISS THE ADDED ENJOYMENT OF READING THE ORIGINAL, OBTAINABLE AT YOUR SCHOOL OR PUBLIC LIBRARY.

JULES VERNE

WHEN Jules Verne was a young boy, he once wrote, "I want to go adventuring in strange places—places with palm leaves and red and green birds and feathery ferns taller than men, growing in mysterious jungles and caverns that no one has ever explored, with echoes and secret passageways."

Verne's love of adventure caused him to run away from home when he was a boy. He paid a cabin boy on a ship to change places with him. He sailed off hoping to see all the wonderful places he had dreamed about. But life aboard ship was not as exciting as he thought it would be. He had to spend most of his time below deck serving food to the crew, clearing tables and washing dishes. When the ship reached a port, his father was there to take him home. The boy was relieved.

Verne spent his childhood in Nantes, France, where he had been born on February 8, 1828. He was very imaginative and liked to amuse himself and his friends by drawing pictures and plans of things considered very strange then, such as horseless carriages driven by steam. He was also athletic and he enjoyed walking around on stilts.

Verne liked to write adventure stories and plays but did not tell his father about them because he knew he would not be pleased. His father was a very successful lawyer and he wanted his son to be a lawyer, too. When Verne was sixteen, he began to study law in his father's office.

When he was ready to take his first law examination, he went to Paris. He passed the examination and went back home. But he decided that one day he would return to Paris to live and write.

In November, 1848, he made a second trip to Paris for another law examination. This time he met Alexandre Dumas and the two men became friends. Dumas read Verne's plays and decided to produce one. This was very exciting for Verne and gave him the encouragement he needed.

Even though he passed his law examination, he wrote to his father, "I am not coming home, I am going to devote myself to literature. I may become a good writer, but I would never be anything but a poor lawyer."

Life in Paris was a struggle for Verne. In order to earn money, he gave lessons to young law students. He worked hard at his writing but did not achieve any success at first. He married in 1857 and it was difficult for him to support his wife, who was a widow with two children.

Finally, in 1863, with the publication of *Five Weeks in a Balloon,* he became famous. The book was very popular and Verne was hailed as an outstanding young author.

After that, he wrote many books including *Around the World in Eighty Days, From the Earth to the Moon, A Journey to the Centre of the Earth, Michael Strogoff* and *Twenty Thousand Leagues Under the Sea.*

Before Verne wrote a book, he read everything he could find on the subject about which he was going to write. He had a great deal of imagination, which made him a master at science fiction. He predicted the invention of the incandescent bulb, the submarine and the electric clock, among other things.

He was honored by the French Academy and received the Legion of Honor medal for his writings. He died, prosperous and successful, in 1905.

Themes

A JOURNEY TO THE CENTRE OF THE EARTH: INTRODUCTION

By WILLIAM B JONES JR 2008

Author of Classics Illustrated: A Cultural History

The science in *A Journey to the Centre of the Earth* may be askew, but Jules Verne's fiction never fails to enthral the reader in this extraordinary voyage. The novel, published in 1864, was the second of the author's *Voyages Extraordinaires*, as his editor Jules Hetzel called the long series of "scientific romances" that was launched in 1863 with *Five Weeks in a Balloon*. Hetzel proclaimed that the intent of the body of Verne's work was "to outline all the geographical, geological, physical, and astronomical knowledge amassed by modern science and to recount, in an entertaining and picturesque format ... the history of the universe."

It was a tall order, but the author did his best to fill it in more than sixty works of unsurpassed imaginative power. In 1864, following the success of his initial airborne adventure, Verne headed in the opposite direction, below the earth's surface in *Voyage au Centre de la Terre*, as his *Journey* is known in French. It became one of the author's best-loved works. The scientific foundation of the novel rested on rather shaky ground. For fictional purposes, at least, Verne subscribed to the theories of his friend Charles Saint-Claire Deville, who argued that European volcanoes were connected by subterranean passages, and the American John Cleves Symmes, who maintained that the earth was hollow with five concentric spheres opening at the North and South Poles. Louis Figuier's *La Terre avant le deluge* (1863) provided background for many underground scenes.

Verne scholar William Butcher has noted the literary influences of Edgar Allan Poe, Alexandre Dumas and George Sand among others on *A Journey to the Centre of the Earth*. Indeed, Verne drew so heavily from Sand's novel about the exploration of the interior of the earth – eg, the appearance of prehistoric animals and the absence of heat at the centre – that she remarked on the similarities in her diary. Another writer, Leon Delmas, unsuccessfully sued Verne, claiming that he had lifted certain plot elements from his short story, *La Tete de Mimers*.

In Verne's novel, an eccentric German professor, Otto Lidenbrock, and his nephew Axel, the narrator of the story, set forth on "the strangest expedition of the nineteenth century". Accompanied by their Icelandic guide Hans and outfitted with practical tools and scientific instruments (carefully enumerated by the author), they follow a 16th-century alchemist's mysterious directions and descend into the mouth of an inactive volcano in their quest to reach the centre of the earth.

As in all quest stories, the journey itself is more important than the accomplishment of the objective. What gives meaning to Professor Lidenbrock's undertaking is a sustained testing of mind, body and spirit that constitutes the very essence of the expedition. As a result of the experience, the young narrator Axel attains an intuitive understanding of one's place in the grand pattern of the evolution of the universe. In a visionary waking dream, he evokes the various stages of the earth's development, concluding with the imagined mingling of his own being "like an imponderable atom with the vast body of vapour which described its flaming orbit in infinite space!"

When *A Journey to the Centre of the Earth* was published in 1864, the Darwinian revolution had been underway for only five years. Axel's rhapsody on the evolving earth suggests something of the direction of mid 19th-century scientific thought. Ironically, however, the theoretical basis of the novel's central premise – that one could indeed travel to the centre of the earth – had become widely discredited by the time the novel appeared. But the flawed thesis regarding the nature of the earth's core in no way compromised the exciting tale that Jules Verne told.

Further notes by Howard Hendrix.....

Verne referred to *A Journey to the Centre of the Earth* as a "scientific romance" – what was meant by this?

Romance

When we hear the word "romance" today, we are apt to think of a novel, story or film dealing with a love affair but the romance was often a long medieval narrative in prose or verse describing the adventures of chivalric heroes – of knights and their ladies. These adventures often took the form of quests wherein the knight proved himself worthy of a lady's love. A romance later came to mean any long work of fiction that described heroes encountering extraordinary or mysterious events.

A Journey to the Centre of the Earth harkens back to one of the oldest stories of romance, the myth of the Fisher King. The Fisher King story, in its earliest versions, involves a young knight who enters a troubled kingdom ruled by a king who is wounded, weak or otherwise failing. The knight is presented with a quest – a dangerous mission in which he must overcome obstacles, acquire wisdom, receive his initiation into the world and return triumphant. If he is successful the Fisher King and his kingdom will be healed and the young knight will win the hand of the King's daughter and eventually come to rule the Kingdom himself.

In *A Journey to the Centre of the Earth* the Professor's house is on Konigstrasse – King's Street. Professor Lidenbrock is rich but his house is ramshackle and overgrown and he is something of an unrecognised genius. Axel's mission is to help the Professor accomplish his journey into the underworld and thereby help the Professor gain the recognition he deserves. Axel's prize for doing so will be the hand in marriage of the Professor's niece and God-daughter, Grauben. Axel accomplishes this mission: the young man makes the descent and return, the Professor gains the reputation he deserves, Grauben marries Axel and they live in the house on King's Street.

Verne's romance, then, is definable as "a long fiction that describes heroes encountering extraordinary or mysterious events" but it still retains echoes of the earliest meaning of romance.

Science

Just as in the traditional romance, myth and religion served as the source of authority for the story, science (and sometimes pseudoscience) serves as the source of authority for Verne's romance. *A Journey to the Centre of the Earth* is full of references to scientific instruments – thermometer and chronometers, compasses, coils and batteries – as well as to numerous fields of science: mineralogy, meteorology, biology, palaeontology and psychology.

Science provides the authority for virtually all the marvels Lidenbrock, Axel and Hans encounter on their journey. "When science has spoken", Lidenbrock says, "we must be silent". He also says "Facts overcome all arguments" – just as his predecessor Saknussemm finishes his note with the authoritative statement "I did it". Yet Verne's relationship to the sciences of his day was hardly one of total agreement. The idea that humans were giants in the past but have since "shrunk" falls closer to devolution than evolution and Verne's giant, hairy mammoth-herder sounds more like a Yeti or a Sasquatch or some other type of Big Foot than any human ancestor.

Verne's fascination with great stretches of space and time and with something like biological and cosmological evolution is evident in *A Journey to the Centre of the Earth* — particularly in Axel's time-travelling dream sequences. But this evolution owes more to Cuvier and Saint-Hilaire (both pre-Darwinian naturalists) than it ever owed to Darwin. As a devout Roman Catholic, Verne believed that Darwinian evolution and scripture were irreconcilable. Verne's vague belief in evolution and Geological antiquity was always linked to his own believer's interpretation of the Genesis account of creation — an interpretation which held that, in ***Cont'd*** "the scale of animal life...man forms the summit." On evolution and antiquity, as on a number of speculative topics, the novel splits the difference. Even at the end, after all he has seen and experienced, Axel still believes that the accepted theory of a hot centred earth is largely correct.

Neither the intuitive nor the empirical position triumphs completely. This is perhaps a good thing — and it apparently reflects something of the nature of Verne's own thinking. Despite his claims that he was more "scientific" than H. G. Wells, here Verne nonetheless puts his most intriguing scientific speculations into Axel's dreams and visions.

The Descent into the Underworld

The purpose of all the science here, finally, is essentially to clothe an old myth in a new lab coat. That myth is the story of the descent into the underworld, a story previously told by Dante, Virgil and Homer among many others. The popularity of such a story may be that it allows the hero to confront the past — usually a personal, unconscious past of ancestors and acquaintances and repressed memories. In that sense the descent into the underworld is also a descent into the self. What the hero overcomes in accomplishing his mission is another way of talking about what each of us overcomes in creating a whole self.

In the journey to deep underground and back in time that Verne provides us with, we find definite allusions to the classical Hades and the Christian Hell. Verne gives us literal fires and literal monsters, but the underworld here goes far beyond human history. Verne's heroes descend into the unconscious of the entire planet — where species that, in the daylight world, are long extinct and known only through fossil traces, live and thrive. Axel, Hans and Lidenbrock first walk amid the world's petrified and fossilised memories, among species repressed out of existence in the "upper" world — and then among the "living fossils" themselves.

Verne's great success lies in combining the personal time of the protagonists' descent with a dreamlike, universal time in the underworld. If we say that Lidenbrock, Axel and Hans represent respectively the superego, ego and id of a complete psyche, then the plot events of the descent make much more sense. Such a psychoanalytic reading helps explain why Axel spends so much time unconscious, while Lidenbrock and Hans do not. Every time Axel falls into unconsciousness it signals a major transition point of the narrative. When Axel comes to he almost always discovers that Lidenbrock and Hans are still active and that, through their activity, they've solved one or another difficulty while Axel was out.

In psychoanalysis only ego is normally conscious, while superego and id are both unconscious. So if the journey to the centre of the Earth is also a journey into the unconscious, it makes narrative sense that Lidenbrock and Hans should remain active (the unconscious is their world, after all) while Axel should keep slipping out of consciousness — and that it should be while Axel is unconscious that major plot problems get solved.

It also makes sense that, as a result of his collapses and recoveries Axel begins to acquire the traits of both the Professor and Hans: "The zeal of the Professor, his earnest longing for success, had become part and parcel of my being," as Axel describes it. The entire journey into the grave like Earth, in through one volcano and out through another, can be read as a death and rebirth: Axel leaves boyhood and is born into manhood as a result of the journey.

In *A Journey to the Centre of the Earth*, Verne uses the old tale of the descent into the underworld as his basis for combining, in an unprecedented way, the romantic quest for understanding the self and the scientific quest for understanding the world.

That's one interpretation of the book but interpretation is a game more than one can play. Create your own, but remember the game's cardinal rule: you have to be able to prove your interpretation with evidence from the text.